THE ANGRY BIRDS™ MOVIE

HarperFestival is an imprint of HarperCollins Publishers.

The Angry Birds Movie: The Junior Novel
© 2016 Rovio Animation Ltd., Angry Birds, and all related properties,
titles, logos, and characters are trademarks of Rovio Entertainment
Ltd. and Rovio Animation Ltd. and are used with permission.

Library of Congress Control Number: 2015959763
ISBN 978-0-06-245336-5

16 17 18 19 20   OPM   10 9 8 7 6 5 4 3 2 1
❖
First Edition

THE ANGRY BIRDS™ MOVIE
THE JUNIOR NOVEL

ADAPTED BY
CHRIS CERASI

Based on the
screenplay written by
Jon Vitti

HARPER FESTIVAL
An Imprint of HarperCollinsPublishers

PROLOGUE

Way out in the middle of the calm, clear blue sea you will find Bird Island, home to the Angry Birds. Most of the birds lived in Bird Village. And in one particular home in Bird Village lived the triplet blue birds Jim, Jake, and Jay, along with their parents.

One evening, the three blue birds were being tucked into their nest by one of Bird Island's most infamous birds: Red. Red was known as one of the angriest birds on Bird Island. But after some recent events, he'd become one of the island's biggest heroes. In fact, Red was so well liked that he was the honorary uncle to a lot of the hatchlings in Bird Village, especially the triplets. Because of this, their parents called on Red whenever they had a date night.

Jim, Jake, and Jay were no exception, and as Red tucked them into their comfy nest, the Blues begged him to tell them a story.

"Uncle Red," said Jake, "will you tell us a bedtime story?"

"Ooh, yes," said Jay. "Please, Uncle Red!"

Red cringed a little, then ran a wing through the tuft of feathers on his head. He was still getting the hang of babysitting, and storytelling did not come naturally to him. "Sure thing, fellas. What do you want to hear?"

"Tell us about the time you saved Bird Island!" shouted Jim. "I love that story!"

"But you've heard it so many times before. Aren't you tired of it?" asked Red.

All three birds shouted "NO!" at the same time and started giggling.

Red sighed, then sat in a chair next to the Blues' nest.

"Okay, okay," he said. "I'll tell you the story one more time. Ready?"

The Blues nodded and smiled.

"Not that long ago, right here on Bird Island, lived a group of cheerful birds. Almost every bird on the island was happy and content. All except one bird . . ."

CHAPTER 1

Life on Bird Island was always peaceful and happy. How could it not be when the sun was always shining, there was always lots to do and see, and every bird was surrounded by friends and family? They lived on a tropical paradise that was theirs alone. There were no other islands or creatures anywhere in sight. As far as the birds were concerned, the only thing that existed was Bird Island. What else could possibly be out there?! Every bird on Bird Island was perfectly satisfied with island life.

That is, every bird except Red.

Red was not a peaceful bird. Red was not

a happy bird. He was an *Angry* Bird.

Red was angry because none of the other birds were anything *but* happy. They were happy *all the time*, no matter what day it was, where they were, or who they were with. This drove Red crazy.

No bird ever questions anything, he thought. *None of the birds does anything but agree to what everyone else says. No bird does anything different! They're all . . . the same.*

Because Red knew he was different and didn't like that every other bird was the same, he grew angrier and lonelier as time went on. He did not hang out with the other birds, eat with them, or share in their fun. He even lived apart from the other birds, in an isolated hut on the beach far away from the rest of Bird Village.

Red also had a bit of a temper. Once, Red got angry at a bird that was standing too close to him in line at the Early Bird Worms shop and almost punched him. Another time he elbowed a mime in the stomach when he disturbed Red while he was reading. Red was known for chasing young birds away from his house when they made too much noise playing outside his beach hut. He even jammed his popcorn bucket on the head of another bird who sneezed on Red at the movies!

Red felt a little better letting the anger out, but then the yelling would just make him even angrier. Red's bad attitude made him unpopular with the other birds. They were afraid of his temper and avoided him whenever they could. Plus, the birds were very busy with their families and friends, especially their hatchlings.

Bird families were extremely proud and protective of their children, especially those who had not yet hatched. They proudly displayed their unhatched eggs for all to see. It seemed to Red that their lives revolved completely around their eggs!

As much as he didn't like the fact that all the other birds were the same, Red sometimes wondered what it would be like to have friends. But as long as the other birds remained the same, Red stayed just as he was. **ANGRY.**

Red's temper also made it hard for him to keep a job. He was given many chances at many places across Bird Island, but as soon as he got angry, he either quit or was fired. Red was down to his last possible job: a hatchday clown! His job was to deliver hatchday cakes and sing "Happy Hatchday" to young birds all across Bird Island whenever they had a party. This job did not make Red very happy. And, worst of all, he had to wear a costume!

One morning, he was late for a hatchday party for a young bird named Timothy. Timothy and his parents, Edward and Eva, lived on the far side of Bird Island, which took quite a long time to get to. Even though he left his hut in plenty of time, Red ended up running late. He managed to get caught in a massive spider web, almost fall off a cliff, get smacked in the chest with tree branches, and swing through the dense jungle from vine to vine. And that was all before he slipped and fell and landed in a lake, nearly drowning! With each trip, slip, and crash, the cake Red carried got bumped and squashed. Red was too worried about making it to the party on time to stop and check on the cake.

After what seemed like hours, Red finally reached the house belonging to Timothy and his parents. He noticed that there was an unhatched egg sitting cozily in its nest on the porch. *Great,* thought Red. *Another bird I'll eventually have to avoid!*

Red took a moment and looked himself over. He was dirty, wet, and tired, but he had made it. As he brushed himself off and put on his red clown nose and wig, Red hoped Timothy and his parents would appreciate just how much he had gone through to get there. He knocked on the door.

He expected to be greeted by lots of screaming little birds and the sounds of a party in full swing. Instead, the door opened to complete quiet, and Red looked down to see little Timothy looking sad and disappointed.

"Ta-da!" said Red. "Happy Hatchday to you!"

Before Red could get much further, Timothy started screaming. In a panic, Red fumbled for the note he had received about Timothy. Sure enough, written on the note was "Hates clowns."

"Oh boy," sighed Red.

Timothy's father, Edward, came to the door when he heard his son scream, and demanded to know where Red had been and why he was over an hour late. When Red tried to explain that he had had to fight his way through the jungle, Edward held up a wing and told Red that he was making excuses. When Red opened the egg containing the cake, he gasped in horror. The cake was completely smashed, and a squirrel had begun eating part of it!

"This is *your* fault," he shouted at Red. "Stop telling tall tales. Just bird up and take responsibility!"

Red started to get angry. "It wasn't a story. I almost died!"

Edward grabbed the hatchday cake from Red and glared at him. "Why don't we just settle this and say the cake's on you?"

Just then, Timothy's mother, Eva, came outside to see what all the commotion was.

"What's going on here?" she screeched, looking at Red and her husband.

Red's wings curled into fists, but he spoke very calmly. "I'm sure you're not going to like this, but this cake . . . is on YOU!"

With that, Red smashed the hatchday cake into Edward's face! Timothy began to cry again as Edward grabbed Red. The two hit the ground with a loud crash. Cake and feathers went flying everywhere. Red landed on something hard that made a cracking noise. When he looked down, he saw that he had landed on the unhatched egg! It had cracked open, and to Red's horror, a baby bird emerged and smiled at Red.

"Daddy!" the hatchling said happily.

Red swallowed his fear and turned to Timothy, Edward, and Eva. He shrugged his shoulders.

"Uh, congratulations! It's a boy!"

When Eva began crying, Red knew that he was in big, big trouble. . . .

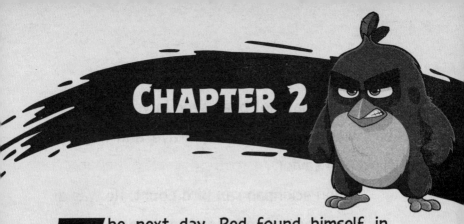

CHAPTER 2

The next day, Red found himself in Bird Court. He would have to answer questions about the hatchday party fiasco. Bird Court sat in the middle of Bird Village and was where birds went whenever they needed to settle a disagreement. Not many birds had disagreements, so having to go to court was a big deal. Red was nervous as Eva began to explain her side of the story.

To make matters worse, behind Bird Court stood a giant statue of Mighty Eagle, the birds' hero and protector. Many years ago, Mighty Eagle had saved the birds from an unknown foe, and now he was a legend. Even though he had not been seen in years, every bird was in awe of their brave and mighty hero and savior.

Judge Peckinpah ran Bird Court. He was a tiny bird who wanted the other birds to think he was large and powerful. Under his flowing judge robes, he stood on top of another bird, Cyrus, so that he could appear taller and more impressive. Even when he was off duty, the judge never appeared anywhere without his robes and without standing on top of Cyrus. Being important—and having every bird think he was important—was Judge Peckinpah's number one priority. He also liked to hear the sound of his own voice. He could not wait for Eva to finish explaining what had happened at the hatchday party so he could begin grilling Red.

Red had been listening to Eva for some

time now and was getting angry. He wanted to defend himself. He knew that this bird family was out to get him.

"We were looking forward to a natural hatching, Your Honor," Eva said dramatically. "There was going to be music and flowers, and the first faces he was going to see were his loving mother's and father's." She looked at Red and narrowed her eyes. "We can never get that moment back!"

Red sighed, then stood and addressed the court. "Ma'am, I never wanted my face to be the first face your baby saw." He looked over at the baby bird, which smiled at Red and shouted "Daddy!"

Red scowled, then continued, "Ladies and gentlemen, am I a passionate person? Yes. Guilty as can be. But I worked very hard to get that cake there on time!" Red pointed at Edward and could barely contain his anger. "And he wouldn't even try it!"

As the crowd whispered to each other in shock, Judge Peckinpah banged his gavel on the desk and turned his attention to Red. Red rolled his eyes. He knew that a boring speech was coming.

"Mr. Red, we are a happy, happy bird community. Under the protection of Mighty Eagle, we work, we play, we laugh, we love. We live our lives free of conflict and strife. So what am I to make of the likes of *you*?" the judge began. "There seems to be a recurring issue here with you, Mr. Red: anger."

"I don't have an anger issue," shouted Red. "You do!"

The judge ignored Red and continued.

"Anger is a weed growing in our garden. And what do you do when you find a weed?"

Red crossed his arms, trying desperately to keep from exploding in anger. "I don't know, but I bet you're going to tell me."

"You pluck it out!" the judge continued as the court gasped in shock. "Mr. Red, given the severity of the crimes, I have no choice but to impose the maximum penalty allowed by the law."

Red's stomach dropped, and he started to get nervous. He leaned forward to hear what Judge Peckinpah was going to say next.

"I hereby sentence you to . . . Anger-management Training classes!"

Red slapped a palm against his face. He couldn't believe it. Not that. Anything but that. Anger-management Training classes

were worse than *anything* Red could think of.
All the anger drained out of him, and he sank
down in his chair.

"Oh no. No no no no no!"

CHAPTER 3

Red sighed in disappointment as he left Bird Court. Anger-management Training classes! He couldn't believe it. Red would rather give up his hut! He had no idea what happened in these classes, but he knew enough about the teacher, a white-feathered bird named Matilda. She was one of the perkiest and most annoying birds on the island: Red shuddered as he imagined all the peppy, perky things Matilda made her students do.

The Infinity Acceptance Center was a place where birds had to go in order to become happier, more relaxed, and stress-free citizens of Bird Island. Judge Peckinpah sent all angry or troubled birds that appeared in his court straight to those classes. With each step, Red was dreading the thought of spending time with Matilda.

Matilda was a former Angry Bird. But after going through anger-management therapy of her own, she decided to open a place where she could help other birds get rid of their anger. She was cheerful, happy, and positive *all the time.* Red could not be more different from any other bird on the island.

As he walked by the Early Bird Worms shop, Red passed the always-happy Stella, who waved at him. "Hey, Red, how are you?"

"Oh, I'm horrible," Red said as he passed on by. He walked by lots of other shops, all of which were bustling with happy, cheerful birds. He pushed through happy bird families out for a stroll and a street performer playing a cheerful song. Everywhere he looked, Red saw nothing but happy birds. He ignored them all and kept walking.

Eventually he came to Matilda's hut, also known as the Infinity Acceptance Center. Red stared at a silly-looking dummy that swayed in the breeze in front of her hut. It was *supposed to* look like a bird. Red thought it looked ridiculous. The dummy held several signs that read Be Happy, Smile, and Welcome, Angry Birds! The more Red looked at the dummy, the angrier he got. He tried to calm himself down and took a deep breath. As he walked by the dummy, he gave it a little push.

The dummy bounced back and hit him on the head. Red snapped. "You think that's funny, huh?" Red grumbled. "*This . . . this* is funny!" he shouted as he grabbed the dummy and spun it around. He let go of it, and the dummy went flying. It crashed into Matilda's hut. Red smiled and dusted off his wings. As he made his way up the steps, he tripped and fell. Red swore he could have heard the dummy laughing at him.

Red brushed himself off and entered Matilda's hut. It was filled with posters and statues of smiling birds, hugging birds, and birds in various yoga poses. He spotted a framed picture of Matilda receiving a certificate that was hanging next to the certificate itself, which read "Free-Rage Chicken."

"Oh, this is gonna be awful," he said to himself.

"Hi there, and welcome to the Infinity

Acceptance group" came a voice from behind him. Red turned and stood beak-to-beak with Matilda, who continued talking. "I'm Matilda, and I'm just super-psyched to be taking this journey with you! You're going to have a blast! I'm really fun. Everybody says that!"

Matilda grabbed Red's wing and led him into the next room, where several birds sat on cushions in a circle on the floor. "Hey, guys! Say hello to Red."

"Hello, birds I won't get to know well," said Red.

"Hi, Red! I'm Bomb," said a big black bird with a big smile.

Before Red could respond, a hyper yellow bird began waving frantically at him.

"Apparently somebody didn't get the memo that we like to start on time, because you're about two minutes late, don't let it happen again. Hi, my name is Chuck, I'm sorry we got off on the wrong foot, I like you a lot, I can tell!"

Red just stared at Chuck, as he could not believe how fast the yellow bird had talked! Matilda led Red into the circle and made him sit on a cushion.

"Now, Red, would you like to share your story with us?" she asked.

"No, not really," he replied.

"The court mentioned something about a rage episode at a child's hatchday party," Matilda said.

Great, thought Red. *She knows.* "So, how long is this class anyway?" he asked.

"You are here until I notify the court that your anger issues have been resolved," said

Matilda. When she saw Red's face fall, she turned to Chuck. "Chuck, why don't you share your story with Red."

Chuck sat up straight and pointed to his chest. "I'm the last guy who should be here. Simple speeding ticket! Judge tells me I was going too fast, so I say, 'Your Honor, to be honest, I was. You caught me. I'm not angry. I'm honest. So shouldn't I be in honesty-management class?'"

Matilda looked at Chuck and shook her head. "That's a different story from the one you told last time. Why don't you tell everyone what really happened."

"Okay, sure. So, I got pulled over for running through a stop sign, and while I was waiting for that very slow police bird to write me a ticket, I may have run to his office and messed up all his papers and the pictures and diplomas on his wall, then stolen his wallet and treated everyone at the coffee shop, then bought some ice cream, which I . . . accidentally . . . dropped on his face. All while he was still writing me a ticket."

Matilda looked at Chuck disapprovingly, but he just shrugged his shoulders.

"What was I supposed to do? He was taking *forever*, and I can't help it if I move really, really, really fast! Like, super-amazingly wonderfully incredibly fast."

After Chuck finished, Matilda introduced Red to another bird. A very, very, very large bird with dark-red feathers named Terence.

Terence just growled at Red in response to being introduced, and Red said, "More like Ter-rifying!"

As Matilda looked through Terence's folder, her eyes widened, then she shut the folder quickly. "Terence seems to have had an . . . um . . . incident. Uh, anyway, this is Bomb," Matilda said, pointing to the black bird who had introduced himself earlier to Red.

"Bomb started with us two weeks ago," continued Matilda. "Tell us your story, Bomb."

"Okay. Well, sometimes when I get upset, I have been known to blow up."

"So you get mad?" Red asked.

"No," replied Bomb. "I literally blow up. I explode. Like a bomb. Hence the name. I have what's known as Intermittent Explosive Disorder."

"We call that IED in my profession," said Matilda helpfully.

"Yeah, that. The worst was when I came home on my last bird-day to find that several friends had thrown me a surprise party. When they jumped out and shouted 'Happy bird-day,' I got so scared I blew up. Total party foul. So yeah, I explode a lot."

Chuck jumped up and down, shouting, "Do it!"

"No can do," said Bomb. "I just went boom-boom before class."

"Do it!" Chuck shouted again.

"Not the time or place, little amigo," Bomb said.

Before Chuck could pester Bomb any further, Matilda stood up in front of the class. "Today we're going to be working on managing our anger through movement. Everybody up!"

"Great," muttered Red under his breath. He reluctantly stood up with the other birds.

A few minutes later, Matilda was leading the birds through a series of yoga poses. Red and a few of the others struggled to keep up. Bomb shook and started to sweat. Chuck was doing his own thing and working his way quickly through one pose after another.

"The first pose is the Dancer pose," said Matilda. "Does anyone know what comes next?"

"I do!" shouted Chuck. "Eagle! Heron! Peacock! Warrior! Mountain! Tree! Rabbit! Fish! Locust! King Pigeon! Downward Duck!"

Red was about to make a remark to Chuck when he noticed Bomb sweating and shaking even more. Red began to get very worried.

"Uh, excuse me, boring hippie lady, but it looks like the explode-y guy is gonna puke."

Matilda walked over to Bomb and noticed that his eyes were beginning to tear and that he was having trouble keeping still. "And how are we doing over here, Bomb?"

"Doing wonderful," Bomb gasped. "Stretching out the core."

"Just remember to breathe," said Matilda. "Up through your feathers and from your talons."

Suddenly, Bomb's eyes widened, and Matilda realized what was about to happen next. She closed her eyes and waited for the inevitable BOOM. Bomb exploded and blew the roof off Matilda's hut.

"Nice!" shouted Chuck as he looked around

at the damage. Not only had the roof been blown clean off Matilda's hut, but the walls were charred and black. Smoke billowed up from the hut. And all the birds were covered in ash and bits from the roof. Matilda decided it was probably enough for the day and dismissed the class early.

Red, Chuck, and Bomb walked back to Bird Village after leaving Matilda's hut. Bomb was still smoking a little from his explosion.

"So where are we going now?" Chuck asked.

"We?" Red asked in return, looking uncomfortable. "Uh, well, you know, I got a thing."

"A thing?" gasped Chuck. "Like a disease?

Bird flu? Chicken pox? Cardinal sin?!"

"No, by 'thing' I mean I don't want to hang out . . . with you."

"Oh," said Chuck. He was very disappointed and a little hurt, but he pretended not to be. "Yeah, well, I've got something, too. How did I forget?"

Bomb felt bad for Chuck and joined in as well. "I'm busy tonight, too. I have . . . a business offer deal . . . thingy. . . ."

"Okay," said Red. "Good." With that, he turned and left Chuck and Bomb standing in the middle of the street.

"Looks like it's just us," said Bomb. "Wanna get a bite to eat?"

"Sure," said Chuck. At least he knew Bomb was his friend, and that made him feel a lot better.

✳ 🌀 ✘ 🌀 ✳

When Red got home, he sat at his table and picked up a model of his hut he had built. He wanted to make the hut bigger but still keep it separate from all the other huts. That had always been the idea.

At least, that was the way he had wanted it and planned for it up until tonight. As he looked at the other birdhouses in the distance and saw lots of lights and heard lots of laughing, he felt alone. Suddenly his hut seemed very small and very far away. Being alone had always been fun before, but tonight, it did not feel like much fun at all.

CHAPTER 4

The next day at Anger-management Training class, Matilda had every bird read a poem they had written about their feelings. Bomb had just finished reading his when Matilda called on Red to read his poem. But Red had not written a poem. He felt it was a waste of his time. Just as Matilda started to get upset, Chuck raised his wing to read his poem.

"My poem is about a hate crime against Billy," he began, and took out the dummy Red had smashed to pieces the day before. Red knew he was in trouble when Chuck showed everyone a red feather he'd found by the smashed-up dummy. It must have gotten stuck to the dummy when Red was beating it up!

"Uh-oh," said Red.

Chuck looked at Red in disgust as he read his poem:

"OH, BILLY!

WHAT COULD HAVE MADE HIM SO DESPISE

YOUR HAPPY SMILE, YOUR LAUGHING EYES?

YOUR SOUL WAS PURE, YOUR HEART WAS TRUE,

AND SOMEONE HATED THAT. BUT WHO?"

Red realized that Chuck had made the dummy! Red was about to respond when Matilda interrupted.

"Billy has passed on to a higher plane of existence. Everyone join wings. Let's say our good-byes."

All the birds joined wings, but they did not let Red join the circle. He did not try to push his way in. After Chuck said a few words, Red tried to apologize.

"Listen, Chuck, I'm really so—"

"What's going on?" Bomb interrupted as he noticed a commotion going on outside Matilda's hut. Birds were running past toward the beach.

"Hey, where's everybody going?" he asked.

A bird looked in the window of Matilda's hut. "Hurry! Something's happening at the beach!"

"Last one to the beach is a rotten egg!" shouted Chuck as he took off at super-fast speed.

"Let's go!" chimed in Bomb, and the group left Matilda's hut.

When they got to the beach, Chuck was already waiting, along with dozens of other birds. They were pointing at a ship in the distance that was getting closer and closer by the minute.

"What is that?" asked Red. He could tell by the other birds' expressions that they were wondering the same thing.

The ship got closer. A green flag flapped in the breeze. The birds began climbing over one another to get a better look at the ship.

Just then, the ship hit a rock and changed course. It began picking up speed. Red realized that the ship was heading directly toward his hut! He ran toward his home, but it was too late. The ship reached shore and stopped just as it touched Red's hut. Red breathed a sigh of relief. But then a large anchor dropped from the ship and crashed right through his roof! It smashed through the walls and floors with a loud crash. Red was in shock.

"My house!" cried Red. "My house, my house! That took me five years to build." And just like that, Red's shock turned into anger. Red-hot, boiling anger.

Chuck sped up to Red and glared at him.

"Wow. It's such a shame when you create something and someone just destroys it," he said sarcastically.

Red knew Chuck was still upset about Billy, but all he could do was stare at his damaged hut.

None of the other birds were paying attention. They were too busy staring as a huge door on the side of the ship opened. A motorized gangplank was lowered.

A large pig appeared at the top and looked out over the crowd. He was completely green and round. He had a black beard that made him look very important. A smaller, hairless pig stood next to him, holding a remote control in his hooves. The bearded pig spread his arms and addressed the birds.

"Greetings from my world, the world of the pigs!" he shouted.

The birds all gasped in awe. They'd never heard the word "pig," much less seen one. Then the pig made his way down the gangplank. Or rather, tried to make his way down. As he got halfway, the motor stopped and became stuck.

"Unbelievable," he said, and looked at the other pig, who fiddled with the remote control. The gangplank jerked and began moving him backward to the top of the ramp.

"Wrong way!" he shouted. "We practiced this a hundred times," he said, grabbing the remote out of the other pig's hooves. He fiddled with a few controls and then smiled at the birds. "We're going to come in again."

With a shudder, the gangplank moved forward smoothly, and he descended toward the beach.

"My name is Leonard, but my friends call me Leon," he said warmly. He pointed to the other pig who was standing behind him.

"This is my first officer, Ross. We mean no harm. We saw your island across the sea and thought, 'Wonder what they're up to?'"

As the birds began whispering among themselves, Leonard continued.

"We come from a place called Piggy Island,

and we have sailed everywhere. Two brave souls against the sea. *Just us two."*

"Excuse me," said Red angrily. "Have you come to smash all our houses, or just mine?"

As the other birds gasped in horror at Red's rudeness, Leonard just smiled.

"That's okay. Please don't be afraid; we request the honor of your friendship!"

Ross started to hand out gift baskets. Then he made his way among the birds. He gave each bird a tight hug and called them "friend." When he got to Terence, he realized that maybe a hug wasn't the best way to meet this new pal.

Judge Peckinpah stepped forward and addressed both Leonard and the birds.

"Welcome to Bird Island! Welcome to our new friends, the pigs! Let us have a celebration!"

"Put 'er there," said Leonard as he shook the judge's wing.

The other birds clapped and cheered at this historic moment. Red did not join in. As he watched the birds welcome Leonard and Ross, he could not help but feel that something was off with the pigs.

CHAPTER 5

That evening, Red sat at a table by himself in the great banquet hall used by the birds for special occasions. It was one of the largest structures on Bird Island, with rows of tables and booths that curved down toward a large stage that was used for shows and other special entertainment. Onstage a show put on by the birds for the pigs was wrapping up. It was a song-and-dance spectacular arranged and choreographed by Stella, a perky pink bird. She was in charge of hospitality on Bird Island. Some birds were playing instruments, while Stella and the other dancing birds finished their dance to cheers and claps from the audience.

Sitting alone, Red watched Leonard and Judge Peckinpah chatting and laughing at their own special table. His eyes narrowed. He was still angry about his hut, and Leonard seemed too friendly and eager to impress the birds. Something didn't feel right. Just then, Chuck and Bomb arrived.

"Oh, we meet again," said Chuck coolly.

"Look, Chuck, I can be a jerk sometimes. You made something happy. I couldn't deal with that sign. I was angry and took it out on Billy. I'm sorry about that." Red patted the empty chair next to him. "Here, come on, sit down."

Chuck smiled and sat down next to Red. Bomb squeezed in on the other side of Red. The three new friends watched Leonard and

Ross dance along with some of the other birds. Red noticed that Leonard was in the center of it all. The birds were watching and admiring him and his moves. He just seemed so fake to Red, but why could none of the other birds see that? Red stared at Leonard until he couldn't stand it any longer and sighed.

"You don't like them very much, do you?" asked Chuck. "Why?"

Red didn't hold back. "For starters, they don't have feathers; they're just walking around naked! And we're supposed to be okay with this?"

"That part of them I really admire," responded Chuck. He did not look disturbed at all.

Before Bomb could weigh in with his

thoughts, Leonard took the stage and addressed the birds.

"Thank you for your kindness and hospitality. You have shared with us the wonders of your simple little island. Now we would humbly love to share some of the wonders of our world," he said.

Red crossed his arms and harrumphed.

On the stage, Leonard continued. "A hundred years from now everyone will ask, 'How did the friendship between the pigs and the birds start?'"

"Who cares?" said Red a little too loudly. Chuck covered his face as some of the birds gasped at Red's rudeness.

"To mark this special occasion, your friends the pigs give you . . . the trampoline!" said Leonard.

Two pigs appeared, dragging the trampoline onto the stage, then set it up. It looked to be sloppily built and not very sturdy. Rickety pieces of wood were nailed together and covered by some fabric that had been patched together with uneven stitches.

Next several more pigs appeared. They were wearing bright gymnastic outfits that were very tight. They started jumping up and down on the trampoline. They laughed and giggled uncontrollably.

As the birds started clapping, Red realized something wasn't making sense.

"Wait, I thought there were supposed to be only two of these guys," he said, scratching his head. Neither Chuck nor Bomb noticed that there were more pigs.

As the gymnasts finished their act,

Leonard had another surprise in store.

"My friends, that's not all! Throwing things just got a whole lot easier," he said excitedly. "Say hello to . . . the slingshot!"

The birds oohed in anticipation as the slingshot was brought onstage. It was a big wooden contraption in the shape of a rounded *Y.* It had a large elastic band attached to it. The assistant pigs demonstrated the slingshot by placing baskets of fruit on the band, pulling it back, and then letting go. Fruit flew into the audience, gobbled up by the cheering birds. They were all mesmerized by the slingshot— except for Red. He was growing angrier by the second. He stood up at the table and shouted at the other birds.

"Guys, it's the same fruit that's been sitting in front of you all night! There's nothing special about it! Can't you see that?!"

"I dunno," said Bomb as he swallowed some pineapples and grapes. "It tastes more exciting to me."

Chuck gulped down some bananas and apples. "I agree! I think thrown fruit is the best kind of fruit!"

Red couldn't believe it. How could no one see that these pigs were weird and up to something?

As the birds' clapping died down, Leonard continued his presentation.

"And now, for our last gift to you—"

"Shut up and fix my house!" Red shouted. He couldn't take it anymore.

Several birds shot angry looks at Red. Chuck turned to them and shrugged his shoulders.

"We don't know him," he said quietly to the audience.

Leonard narrowed his eyes at Red. He'd had his fill of Red.

"I'm going to ask for a volunteer from the audience," said Leonard, looking directly at Red. "How about the red guy with the big eyebrows?" He pointed at Red.

Red's eyes widened, and he sunk down in his seat.

"Me? Oh, no no no. . . ."

"Yes, you, sir! Come on up here! It's your lucky day!" taunted Leonard.

The birds started applauding. They urged Red to get on the stage. Chuck and Bomb cheered Red on as well, but Red was not having any of it.

"Are you sure you don't want to choose

any of the other birds?" he asked.

"Come on, Red," said Chuck. "Have some fun."

"Oh, you've got to be kidding me," said Red as he was pushed toward the stage. He knew he was going to regret this. Ross took Red by the arm and led him to the slingshot. Several other pigs joined him and positioned Red directly in front of the elastic band. Red tried to squirm free, but the pigs held him tight in their grip.

"Ready," began Leonard as Red braced himself. "Aim. . . . Fire!"

Before Red realized what was actually happening, he was soaring through the air above the crowd of birds and back toward the beach in the distance.

"This seems really unnatural!" he screamed

as he flew past the other birds.

Leonard smiled and put his hooves on his hips.

"Who says birds don't fly?"

The birds leapt to their feet and began cheering and applauding.

A few long seconds later, Red came crashing into the sandy ground by the beach. He picked himself up and shook his head clear.

"Don't worry, I'm fine! Thanks for the lift!" he shouted back at the party going on in the distance. "Unbelievable."

Red noticed how quiet and lonely it was on the beach this far away from the village. For some reason, it seemed particularly lonely tonight. Maybe it was because he had never felt so apart from everyone before. It was one thing when it was just him and his fellow birds. Now that these pigs were here, it only made him feel less connected to the birds and more on his own. How could none of the other birds see that these pigs were acting odd? It just didn't make sense, and this made Red something worse than mad.

It made him sad.

As Red dusted himself off, he realized he had landed right by the pigs' ship. Just as he was thinking about what to do next, a yellow blur rocketed toward him. Before he could blink, Chuck was standing right next to him. *Wow, he really is amazingly fast,* thought Red.

"You know you want to search their

boat," Chuck said with a smile.

"What? No, I don't," said Red, and then realized he actually wanted to search the boat. "Yeah, you're right. I do."

"Bomb's on his way," said Chuck as the two birds walked toward the ship.

A short time later, Red, Chuck, and Bomb were climbing aboard the pigs' ship. Red reached the deck first, and called back to Chuck and Bomb.

"C'mon, let's go. And remember—keep it quiet! I don't want the pigs alerted. I just know they're up to no good."

Chuck started zipping around the deck in a yellow blur.

"Whoa, this is an impressive ship!" Chuck said loudly.

Red held a wing to his beak to quiet Chuck.

"Inside voice!" he whispered. "Come on. . . ." He motioned Chuck and Bomb inside.

The three birds began searching the ship, opening any closed doors they encountered along the way. One room was filled with trampolines just like the one the pigs gave to the birds. They kept exploring.

Chuck pulled a curtain open. Behind it were several strange-looking vehicles. The birds could not make sense of these machines, so they moved on.

Next Red opened another door. Inside was a massive closet where dozens and dozens of brightly-colored cowboy outfits hung in rows. There were cowboy hats, boots, and bandanas on the shelves.

Red scratched his head. "Who *are* these weirdos?" he asked. Not only were these pigs probably up to something, they were also downright strange.

Red and Chuck heard laughter coming from another room. They followed the noise and found Bomb inside. He was jumping up and down on some trampolines. Red tried to get him to stop, but Bomb broke through a trampoline and went crashing through the floor!

Red and Chuck peered over the edge of the hole Bomb had made to see where their friend had gone. Bomb had landed in another room below. But he wasn't alone. The room was *filled* with pigs. Dozens and dozens of pigs. As Red, Chuck, and Bomb looked at one another in surprise, one of the pigs giggled and said, "We were hiding!"

By the time Red, Chuck, and Bomb returned to the banquet hall, the party was still going strong. The three friends brought the pigs, now dressed in their cowboy outfits, with them. Red was determined to get to the bottom of who these pigs were and what they wanted from the birds. But the noisy party-goers were too busy singing and dancing. Red looked around and climbed on top of the head table to get their attention.

"Hey! Everyone! Everyone! There's more of them!" Red yelled as he pointed to the pigs he, Chuck, and Bomb had brought to the party.

The startled birds stopped singing and dancing, and then looked at Red and the newly-arrived pigs in surprise.

"That's right," Red continued. "I'm back. Enjoying the party? Because while you were living it up, *I* snuck onto their ship!"

The judge looked at Red in shock. "You did what?!"

"And look what I found! There are more of them than we thought. That's mysterious and weird, am I right?" Red pointed at Leonard. "He said there were only two pigs on board, but he was obviously lying."

As the birds turned to look at Leonard, Red paused. He knew the birds were finally listening to him.

"And there are strange devices on their boat, so clearly there's, you know . . . stuff going on. I don't know what stuff, but stuff. Any questions?"

Judge Peckinpah looked shocked. "You snuck onto their ship?"

"I don't need a reward, if you're trying to figure out what honor to bestow on me. I don't need anything." He was feeling satisfied that now the other birds would finally see that the pigs were weird and not to be trusted.

As the birds began to boo loudly, Red kept talking.

"Yeah, boo them! That's right! Wait . . . are you booing them or me?!"

Leonard raised a hoof to silence the crowd.

"Perhaps I can explain," he began, pointing at the pigs. "My cousins are simple folk. They don't even know the alphabet! They just want to perform. I didn't want to risk their lives until I found out if you were all friendly and this was a safe space." Leonard looked at his fellow pigs in their cowboy outfits. "We were going to put on a cowboy show for you, but perhaps it wasn't meant to be. It is not yet time."

As the birds stared in wonder at Leonard, the bearded pig finished his speech.

"I believe that birds and pigs are meant to be friends, but if we crossed boundaries that we shouldn't have . . ."

Leonard choked up before he could finish his thought and then began to cry. The birds all turned and glared at Red. Judge Peckinpah marched up to him and waved a wing in Red's face.

"You've shamed not only yourself," he said coldly, "but our entire community."

Bird Island, a beautiful island in the middle of the sea, is home to a close-knit community of happy birds who live in Bird Village.

Red's short fuse lands him in court, where he is sentenced to anger-management classes.

Well, *almost* all the birds live in the village—not Red. He lives alone on the beach because he gets annoyed by the other birds. Then he gets angry. And then he gets into trouble.

The anger-management classes are held at the Infinity Acceptance Center. Everything about the place ruffles Red's feathers, especially Matilda, the cheerful bird who teaches the classes.

A former Angry Bird, Matilda knows how to channel her anger into more positive outlets, like yoga and painting, which make Red miserable. But at least he's not alone. Three other Angry Birds are also in the class.

Chuck, a fast-footed bird who talks and moves quicker than anyone, has too many speeding tickets.

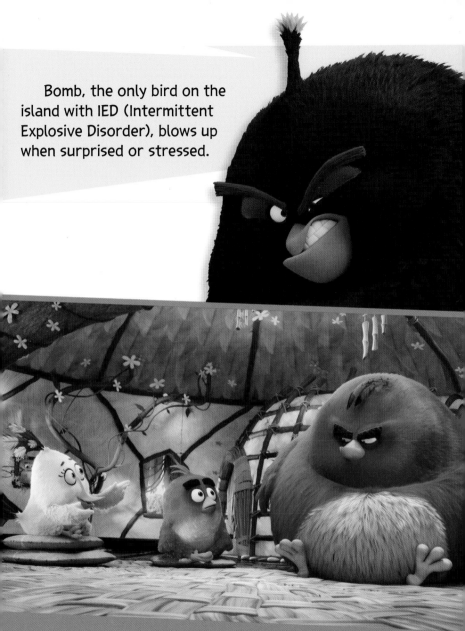

Bomb, the only bird on the island with IED (Intermittent Explosive Disorder), blows up when surprised or stressed.

Terence, the largest of all the birds, spends the day growling and brooding. Only Matilda knows what landed him in her class, and she doesn't want to discuss it.

When a ship of pigs lands on the shores of Bird Island, the birds welcome the happy travelers with open wings and throw a big party.

Soon more ships arrive filled with fun-loving pigs.

The cheerful pigs set up crazy contraptions, like big slingshots, all over the island. Red is not amused.

No one has seen or heard from Mighty Eagle, the legendary hero of Bird Island, in years. But Red wants to find his idol. He is certain Mighty Eagle can solve the pig problem.

"Wait," said Red. "I think you mean 'saved,' not 'shamed,' right?"

"I sent you to treatment to deal with your problems," said the judge. "Clearly more treatment is required!"

"No!" shouted Red and Matilda at the same time.

"Do not trouble our honored guests again!" yelled the judge. He turned to Leonard and put his wing around the pig.

"My friend, we would love to see your cowboy show!"

"Thank you," choked Leonard through his tears. "Thank you so much!"

Judge Peckinpah and the other birds turned away from Red. They rejoined the party with the pigs who had returned to the stage. They had put on their cowboy outfits and were ready to start the show! The entire village, aside from Chuck and Bomb, had turned their backs on Red.

"Whatever, don't listen to me!" he shouted.

Red got his wish—none of the birds were listening to him. This made Red even angrier than he'd been before. Why couldn't they see the same thing that he did? Something was up with these pigs. He was going to get to the bottom of this mystery . . . before something bad happened.

CHAPTER 6

The next morning, Red was grouchier than usual. He'd gotten a terrible night's sleep. His damaged hut gave him no privacy or peace and quiet. All he heard were the happy sounds coming from the cowboy show that had gone on for hours.

Over the next few days, Red noticed that the pigs were taking over Bird Village. Some pigs were teaching the birds how to jump on the trampolines. Other pigs were putting on music shows. And, worst of all, there were pigs lying in the sun, playing volleyball, and swimming on the beach next to his hut!

There were pigs everywhere Red looked.

He could not go anywhere without seeing the pigs taking photos of all the places and things on Bird Island. Red noticed a lot of the pictures were of eggs in nests, as well as eggs used in signs and illustrations.

That's weird, thought Red. *These pigs seem obsessed with eggs! What's so special about ordinary birds' eggs?*

Red wanted to bring it up at Anger-management Training class. But he saw how much the birds and pigs were having fun and getting along, and he knew that it would do no good.

Matilda had the class painting by the beach that afternoon, in a lesson she called "Paint

Your Pain." Red, Chuck, Bomb, and Terence were standing in front of easels, each working on his own canvas. Matilda stood in front of the birds and encouraged them as they painted.

"That's it, class. Feel your pain. Let it out through every brushstroke!" She began walking around each of the birds as they painted. "Thought for the day: water is the softest thing, yet it can penetrate mountains and earth."

Red rolled his eyes. "Here's my thought for the day," he said. "When are we done?"

Matilda sighed. "Red, what the caterpillar calls the end, the world calls a butterfly."

"Can I just say that I never understand a single thing you're talking about?" Red shot back. He slapped more paint on his canvas.

Matilda ignored him and stood next to

Chuck, who was zooming back and forth in front of his canvas. Matilda saw that Chuck was painting himself as a muscled, heroic bird and smiled.

"Wow, Chuck, that's very lifelike."

"What can I say," answered Chuck. "I paint what I see!"

Matilda moved on to Bomb. He had splashed and splattered lots of paint on his canvas—and himself—in a messy explosion. He looked very proud of his painting.

"It's very abstract," said Bomb.

"Okay, yeah," said Matilda, and turned to Terence. "Okay, Terence, let's see your painting!"

If Bomb's had been surprising, Matilda couldn't believe her eyes when she saw Terence's painting. He had painted himself and Matilda touching wings in a very dramatic pose. He grunted his approval as Matilda continued staring.

"Wow, Terence, I did not know you felt that way." Matilda began blushing, then addressed the class. "I think that's probably enough for today. Class dismissed!"

As Red and the others began gathering their things, they saw Stella giving Leonard and some of the pigs a detailed tour on the beach. Judge Peckinpah was standing proudly next to Leonard as Stella recited some facts about the island. Leonard looked bored.

Then Red noticed a change in the big pig. Leonard perked up when he spotted a large bird's egg in a nearby nest. Red said good-bye to Chuck and Bomb and followed the other birds on their tour.

"Is that what I think it is?" asked Leonard excitedly as he ran toward the nest.

"That's an egg," said Stella. "You guys don't lay eggs?"

Leonard sighed but did not tear his gaze away from the egg. "I wish we did," he said. He picked up the egg and squeezed it to his chest.

"Whoa, whoa, whoa, buddy! That is fragile. Maybe you shouldn't pick it up, especially as it isn't yours!" Red said.

"Oh, my friend from the banquet," said Leonard, although he sounded like he thought of Red as anything but a friend. Leonard then looked at the painting Red had been working on, and his eyes widened. "Well, now that's a very good painting."

Red pointed to his canvas. On it he had

painted Leonard getting struck by lightning! "Oh yeah, the assignment was to paint your pain, so I painted *your* pain. I, uh, didn't actually think you were going to see it."

"Wonderful likeness," snorted Leonard. He turned to Stella. "I thought you said you stored your nuts for winter," he said, and began to laugh.

Red was just about to launch another insult at Leonard, but something stopped him in his tracks. He looked out to sea and saw another ship. It was full of pigs and heading right for Bird Island. *Even more* pigs were coming!

"All right, what's going on here?" shouted Red. "Are you explorers, or are you staying? Why are there more of you coming?!"

As Red watched in horror, the second

pig ship crashed into the first one, which destroyed Red's hut even more!

"No! Not my house again! That's my home!"

Judge Peckinpah pulled Red aside. "You're making our guests feel unwelcome!"

"And you're not asking basic questions," replied Red.

"Maybe I wasn't clear enough," Judge Peckinpah sputtered. "Your opinion is not needed. Stay out of this and stay away from our guests!"

As Stella and the birds guided Leonard to the beach to greet the new boatful of pigs, Red stomped away. He walked back into the village and toward Bird Court and the statue of Mighty Eagle. Right now he needed help. Who better to soothe his feathers than Bird Island's greatest hero and protector?

"We could really use you right about now," Red said, staring up at the statue. He sat down at the base of the statue. Suddenly he got an idea about just what to do. But first he needed Chuck's and Bomb's help!

Red headed straight to Chuck's house, which was at the top of a very tall tree. He pulled on a rope that had a bell tied to it, which served as Chuck's doorbell.

"Hey, Chuck, it's Red," he shouted. "Zip on down here!"

Just as Red finished his sentence, there was a blur of yellow, and suddenly Chuck was standing next to Red. He had a mud mask on his face and was sipping a cup of coffee. Red was surprised.

"What's up?" asked Chuck.

"I . . . um . . . have an idea, but I need to

talk to Bomb as well. Want to come along?" said Red.

"Okay," said Chuck. He zipped back up his tree. A split second later he zipped down again, his coffee cup and face mask gone. He was ready.

"Uh, hey, Chuck. What's the deal with the mud mask?" said Red.

"All this does not just happen on its own!" replied Chuck, pointing to his face and body.

They walked to Bomb's hut and knocked on the door. A second later they heard an explosion from within and saw smoke pour out of the windows. Bomb opened the door wrapped in a towel, his feathers still smoking. He looked embarrassed.

"Oh, hey, guys," he said sheepishly. "I was just taking a shower."

"Bomb, buddy, TMI," said Red. "But listen, I have an idea. Come with me."

As Red, Chuck, and Bomb watched the pigs setting up several mysterious construction sites all over Bird Village, Red revealed his idea.

"There's something going on here, and it's up to us to figure it out. Right?"

"Figure out what, exactly?" asked Chuck. He was confused.

As Bomb watched many pigs installing zip lines and nets in several trees, he started to get the feeling Red was right. "It *does* seem a little odd."

"I'll tell you this," said Red emphatically,

"if anyone knows what these pigs are up to, it's Mighty Eagle."

Both Chuck's and Bomb's eyes widened when Red mentioned Mighty Eagle, the legend and hero of Bird Island. Every bird knew all about Mighty Eagle, and every bird had nothing but awe and respect for the noble bird.

"Where does he even live?" asked Chuck.

"By the Lake of Wisdom," responded Bomb in hushed tones. "In the Ancient Tree."

"But that's a fairy tale," Chuck said. "I've been all over this island. Where could it possibly be?"

Red pointed to the giant mountain that rose up in the center of Bird Island and smiled. "Way up high."

Chuck and Bomb turned to look at the

mountain, as Red continued. "It's a long way up that mountain, and if I'm being honest, well . . . I could use your help."

Chuck looked at Red. Was he actually asking *them* for help?

"What's that? What are you trying to say?" Chuck asked. He knew Red was regretting his earlier behavior toward them, and Chuck was savoring the moment.

"I was just saying that I could . . . I could use your help."

"I'm sorry; I couldn't quite hear you over your ego. Could you enunciate that last word a little bit?"

"I need your help!" shouted Red.

"Oh, why didn't you say so? Bomb?"

Bomb smiled at Red and Chuck.

"Let's do it! Let's go find Mighty Eagle!"

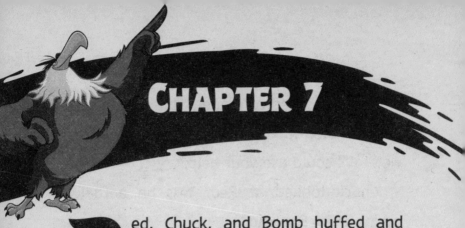

CHAPTER 7

Red, Chuck, and Bomb huffed and puffed through dense jungle, waded through sticky swamps, and climbed up sheer cliffs. The trek was tough, but they just kept going. All three birds were excited and nervous about reaching Mighty Eagle's home. As they climbed, Chuck and Bomb talked about Mighty Eagle's legend. Red tried to stay focused on what he would say once they found his hero.

"If there is a Mighty Eagle, how come we don't ever hear his battle cry?" asked Chuck.

"I don't know," said Red wearily.

"Maybe we have heard it!" added Bomb thoughtfully.

"What would it sound like, do you think?" Chuck wondered. "Something like this? EEH EEH EEH!"

"No, I bet it's more like a CAW CAW CAW!" said Bomb. "That's theoretically more what it's like, scientifically."

"Nah," said Chuck. "I'm thinking maybe it's a little more subtle, a bit more majestic, like SCREEEEEEEEEEEEEEEEEEEEEEE!!!"

Red had kept quiet for hours, but he'd reached his limit. "Stop making Mighty Eagle noises!" he shouted.

"Someone has anger issues," Chuck whispered to Bomb.

Finally, they reached the top of the mountain. The trio couldn't wait to see Mighty

Eagle's home. But instead of a home, they saw Mighty Eagle's mountain in the distance!

Chuck choked back tears. "This . . . this is the wrong mountain!"

"We have to go back down and climb the right one," said Bomb, feeling discouraged.

"My calves are killing me," said Red with a sigh.

All three birds took a deep breath, then began climbing down the mountain they had just finished ascending.

Many hours later, Red, Chuck, and Bomb finally reached Mighty Eagle's mountain and began climbing. Day turned to evening, then night came and went before Red, Chuck, and

Bomb reached the mountaintop. They pulled themselves up and rested to catch their breaths. After a few seconds, they looked around and saw a clear blue lake. A beautiful twisted tree rested on the shore of the lake. It was all very calm and relaxing, and the three birds could not believe they had finally made it to Mighty Eagle's home!

"Wow," said Red as he gazed at the scene before him.

"The Lake of Wisdom!" exclaimed Chuck as he stared into the water. He took a deep sip, and Bomb joined him. Since they were very young, the three friends—along with every other hatchling on Bird Island—had learned all about Mighty Eagle. His daring adventures. His heroic rescues. His commitment to everything fair and just. Seeing the legendary Lake of Wisdom was amazing.

"Be honest," said Bomb. "Do I sound any wiser?"

"Oh, way wiser," agreed Chuck.

Red climbed up the tree and saw an abandoned nest toward the top. It looked like it had not been used in a long, long time. He began to get worried.

"Guys, nobody's here. Nobody's used this place in years," he said. He noticed Chuck and Bomb swimming in the lake. They were swimming, splashing, drinking, and playing in the water. Red felt it was rude to play in the sacred lake.

"What are you doing?" he asked. "Get out of there!"

All three birds paused as they heard a booming echo in the cave that lay above the lake, and Red began to panic.

"Get out! Let's go! C'mon! We should hide!" he warned.

Chuck and Bomb joined Red behind a large rock. They watched as heavy footsteps cut through the still morning air. A large figure emerged from the cave and stood at its entrance. It was Mighty Eagle himself! Red, Chuck, and Bomb couldn't believe it. It was really him!

"Oh wow, it's him," Red whispered in awe. Chuck and Bomb could only stare at the majestic bird, their beaks hanging open.

Mighty Eagle looked a bit older and rounder than Red had expected. But Red still couldn't believe this legend—his hero—was standing right in front of him! Red's awe quickly turned to horror when Mighty Eagle began to relieve himself in the Lake of Wisdom. Chuck and Bomb looked sick when they realized that the water they had been drinking and swimming in was basically Mighty Eagle's toilet! Bomb started to cry, and Chuck began to gag.

"Well," said Red. "It's not so much the Lake of Wisdom as the Lake of Whiz."

Mighty Eagle finished relieving himself and then headed back into his cave. Red, Chuck, and Bomb did not know what to do next. Before they could make a plan, however, Mighty Eagle called back to them over his shoulder.

"Did you come here just to look at me, or did you have something to say?" he asked.

Red, Chuck, and Bomb were shocked—Mighty Eagle had seen them!

The three birds came out from behind

their rock and stood before Mighty Eagle. They all shook a little, nervous about what would happen next.

"You have passed the first test," said Mighty Eagle. "You have found me. Behold! Gaze upon . . . MIGHTY EAGLE! I see all and know all!" He paused for a second.

"What are your names?"

"If you know all, why don't you know who we are?" asked Chuck. Red jabbed him in the side for asking Mighty Eagle such a silly question.

"It's a test of your honesty. I know very well who you are," continued Mighty Eagle. "You are lost souls who have come here seeking wisdom!"

"Can we have some?" asked Chuck eagerly.

"Wisdom is not something that is given. It

is something that is attained."

Bomb looked disappointed. "Oh, okay. Well, good-bye then!"

Mighty Eagle held up a wing. "Will I help you attain wisdom? Yes, that I will do!"

Red stepped forward, and said, "That's great news. By the way, I'm Red, this is Bomb, and this is Chuck. The reason we climbed your mountain is that we want to know—"

Mighty Eagle cut Red off. "Follow me, and prepare to have your minds blown!" he said, before he turned and walked back into his cave.

Red, Chuck, and Bomb shrugged their shoulders and followed the massive bird inside.

After walking down a long, dark tunnel, the four birds emerged into Mighty Eagle's main room. It was large but a little cluttered. Every inch of space on the cave walls was covered with trophies, awards, certificates, and framed photos and newspaper articles featuring Mighty Eagle in his prime. There were a few pieces of ratty, broken furniture here and there. The place looked like it needed a good cleaning.

Mighty Eagle spread his wings and exclaimed, "Welcome to the Hall of Heroism!"

"Well, it's really amazing to meet you," said Red. "I have your poster up in my nest—"

"You might want to shield your eyes from the sparkle of all my trophies!" Mighty Eagle interrupted. "How many do I have? I have no idea. Countless!" He paused a second to think.

"Okay, thirteen." He sat down in a big chair and opened a can of sardines to snack on. Red, Chuck, and Bomb sat on the sofa across from him.

Red decided to get down to business. "So, anyway, the other day, these pigs showed up out of nowhere, and we're concerned that—"

"Would you like to hear my theme song?" asked Mighty Eagle, interrupting Red for the third time. He grabbed a guitar and began singing.

"*Mighty, Mighty Eagle, soaring free, defender of our homes and liberty! Bravery, humility, and honesty!* You must have grown up singing this song in school, yes?" he asked eagerly.

Red played along in the hopes that he could get back to the subject at hand. "Uhhh . . . yeah. Yes, we did."

Mighty Eagle tossed the guitar aside and stood up. It looked like he was getting ready to leave the room, so Red tried to steer the conversation back to the pigs. It was becoming very clear to all three birds that Mighty Eagle was turning out to be not so mighty after all.

"So, about those pigs I mentioned earlier. You see, a second boat arrived and caused me a great deal of suspicion, and . . . he's walking out of the room!"

Red, Chuck, and Bomb could not believe it. Mighty Eagle had just gotten up and left them alone! Maybe tracking down their hero and asking for his help wasn't such a great idea.

"I don't get this," Red said angrily. "This guy just sits here, all alone, and clearly doesn't leave the house. He doesn't care about anyone but himself!"

"Sounds a lot like you," Chuck said quietly.

"Thank you for your opinion, Chuck," said Red. But he realized that Chuck was probably right. Red got up from the sofa and went after Mighty Eagle. He found the older bird staring through a pair of binoculars at Bird Village way below them.

"Hello, Mighty Eagle?" he said as he approached the big bird. "Listen . . . are you going to help us or not?"

Mighty Eagle lowered the binoculars and looked at Red.

"I *am* helping you!"

"No, you're not! You're just singing dumb songs and telling dumb stories and looking through these," Red said angrily as he grabbed the binoculars from Mighty Eagle.

Red looked down at Bird Village with the binoculars. He couldn't help but notice a massive tent in the middle of Bird Village. *Where did that come from?* Red took another look. Dozens of pigs were running in and out of the tent. Other pigs were handing out what looked like party invitations to all the birds, and some were zipping around Bird Village in their strange vehicles. When he looked closer, Red saw that the pigs were stacking boxes of TNT all around the village!

"Whoa, whoa, whoa," Red said. This confirmed something he had suspected all along: the pigs were up to something, and it definitely wasn't something good! Red trusted his instincts.

"Oh my—I was right," said Red, concern in his voice. "I knew it! Bomb! Chuck! Get out here, hurry!"

Mighty Eagle looked through the binoculars at the tent and all the pigs and knew something bad was happening. "Uh-oh."

Chuck and Bomb joined Red and Mighty Eagle on the cliff, and Red was certain that he and his friends had to get back to the village as fast as possible. "Mighty Eagle, fly us down there, now!" he pleaded.

"No," said Mighty Eagle softly.

"I'm sorry, *what*?!" asked Red, shocked.

"I don't do that anymore," said Mighty Eagle sadly. "I'm retired. Mostly just tired. Go handle it yourselves. This is everything I've prepared you for." He turned and started heading back into his cave.

Red could not believe it. Mighty Eagle was abandoning them!

"Prepared us for what? Our whole world—everyone we know—is in danger!"

"Yes," replied Mighty Eagle. "So off you go."

Red was fuming. "You know what? I used to believe in you. When I was a kid, I believed nothing bad could ever happen because you were here. But now I see that I was an idiot!"

"I think it's time for you to go," said Mighty Eagle.

"It's really upsetting to me that you're the only bird that can fly, and you're too afraid to do it." Red turned to Chuck and Bomb. "Come on, guys, let's go. We're done here."

The three frustrated and worried birds made their way back down the mountain.

Mighty Eagle stood and watched them for a while. A small smile spread across his face. It was hard for him to let them go. But it had to be done.

Meanwhile Red, Bomb, and Chuck ran down the mountain as fast as they could. They had an island to save!

CHAPTER 8

As Red, Chuck, and Bomb neared the bottom of the mountain, Bomb tripped on a branch and tumbled into Red. Then Red lost his balance and tumbled into Chuck. All three began bouncing and rolling down the mountainside in a big ball, until they finally landed with a crash in a bush at the bottom of the mountain.

The three friends untangled themselves and dusted one another off. They looked around Bird Village. All the birds on the island were partying underneath the big tent the pigs had put up while they were away. Music was blaring, and all the birds were dancing, laughing, and eating. The pigs were playing music and serving food.

None of the birds noticed the boxes of TNT, and they definitely did not see the pigs hiding more of the TNT boxes under the party tent! The birds were too busy having fun.

The pigs began to spread out into the village. They placed TNT in all the houses. They hid more boxes in every shop on Main Street. They moved quickly and left no spot of Bird Island untouched.

Red, Chuck, and Bomb finally made their way through the village, where they discovered something awful. The pigs were stealing eggs from one of the nests next to a village hut. Everywhere they turned, they saw pigs stealing eggs from every nest in the village!

"What's happening?" shouted Red. "Follow them!"

As they ran after the pigs, Red saw that the two ships the pigs had arrived on were already loaded full of eggs. The pigs were taking every last one of them! Red saw Leonard watching the eggs being loaded onto his ship and realized that this had been the shady pig's plan all along. Not wanting to lose a single second, Red turned to Chuck.

"Run back to the party and get the others—now hurry!"

"I'm on it!" said Chuck as he took off at super-fast speed.

"Bomb, we gotta stop them!" said Red as he and Bomb began to run toward the pigs' ships. As they got nearer, one of the crates of TNT exploded nearby, and they had to duck for cover. When the smoke cleared, they saw that the ships were just about full and the pigs were preparing to sail away.

"We gotta get the eggs off the ship!" shouted Red.

In the meantime, Chuck sped into the party tent and tried to get the birds' attention. They were so busy dancing and laughing, not a single bird had heard any of the explosions. Chuck raced to the stage in desperation and jumped up and down.

"Can everybody please stop partying? The eggs are being stolen!"

When that didn't work, he spotted Matilda and ran up to her.

"Matilda, the eggs are being stolen! We need your help!"

"What?!" cried Matilda. "We have to do something!"

They grabbed Judge Peckinpah and told him what was going on in the village and at the beach. Finally, the music was turned off, and Chuck told the crowd of birds about the pigs' plot.

"We have to get back to the beach! Stop dancing and start running!"

As the pigs secured the last of the eggs on their ship, Leonard saw Red and Bomb running toward them.

"Do we have them all?" he asked. "Get

everyone on board. Let's get out of here!"

Red and Bomb were too far away from the ship to climb onto it. Then Red saw a few of the trampolines the pigs had left behind and got an idea.

"Use the trampolines!" he shouted to Bomb. The two birds began hopping from one trampoline to another, getting closer and closer to Leonard's ship. Finally, Bomb reached the platform the eggs were on, with Red following shortly after.

"Untie the ropes and drop the eggs into the water," shouted Red.

Bomb pulled at the ropes, but they would not budge.

"They're too strong," he said. "I can't break them!"

As Red saw Leonard order the pigs to get Bomb off the platform, he shouted to his friend. "Bomb! Blow up the rope!"

Bomb focused and tried to get himself to explode. He knew that the safety of the eggs depended on him. He squeezed his eyes shut and tried to detonate.

"Come on, Bomb, you can do this!" Red said. "Come on, buddy, blow up!"

"I'm trying!" shouted Bomb, but just as he was ready to explode, the pigs used water guns and doused his fuse. They pushed him and Red off the platform and into the water below.

Leonard laughed at the wet birds as his ship sailed farther away.

"Thanks for your hospitality!" he shouted at them, then turned to Ross. "Set sail for Piggy Island!"

✻ ☙ ✦ ☙ ✻

Red and Bomb swam back to shore. They met up with Chuck and the other birds, who had finally reached the beach. Everyone was shocked and sad. Red looked around and saw that the pigs had destroyed all of Bird Village! Every last house and business had been wrecked by the pigs' TNT. Nothing was left but smoking ruins. Not only that, but all the eggs were gone!

Judge Peckinpah walked over to Red. The judge hopped off of Cyrus and stood in front of Red at his normal height. Red had to look down at the judge, which made everything seem more serious.

"Mr. Red," he said sadly, "what do we do now?"

CHAPTER 9

Red was stunned. His mind was racing. Some of the birds had begun to cry. It took him a few moments to realize what Judge Peckinpah was asking him.

"Wait," said Red, surprised. "You're actually asking *me*?"

"You knew, and you tried to tell us," the judge continued. "And we didn't listen. *I* didn't listen. What do we do?"

Red paused again. All the birds were looking at him. They wanted his help. A part of him believed he was the last bird anyone should be looking to for answers. Still, Red knew what had to be done. He took a deep breath.

"I'll tell you what we're going to do," he said. "We're going to get all the eggs back!"

"How are we going to do that?" asked Matilda.

"The pigs already showed us how," Red explained. "They went back to their home, so that's where we're going."

"And how are we going to do that?" asked the judge.

"We're going to build our own boat," said Red. "They stole your kids. No, they stole *our* kids! Who does that? And you know what? I'm a little bit angry about that. No, correction: I'm *really* angry! And I don't think I'm the only one.

"It's time to get angry," Red continued. "It's time to stay angry together. We're getting our kids back, and I don't need any calm, happy birds. I need some *Angry* Birds! Now who's with me?!"

All the birds volunteered to join Red. He smiled. It felt good to work together with his fellow birds.

"Good. Now let's go get our kids back!"

Red and the other birds quickly got to work on the boat they would use to sail to Piggy Island. Red oversaw the construction, with Chuck and Bomb helping where they could.

"Bring me everything that floats," Red instructed his fellow birds. They were all gathering up the pieces of their destroyed village to be used as parts for the boat. One of the pigs' slingshots worked well as a mast. Red smiled as a bunch of the pigs' banners were turned into sails. Everyone was lending a wing, so the ship took shape in no time at all.

When the boat was finished, Red stepped back and took a good look at it. It wasn't as big as the pigs' boat, but everyone would fit on board, and they could even bring a slingshot. Red realized it might come in handy once they tracked down the pigs.

All in all, he was impressed. Red felt proud that the birds realized he had been right about the pigs. But he was prouder of their work on the boat and how everyone was pitching in. It felt good to be part of a team, Red thought.

"It's darn good for a bunch of birds," he said, and then climbed onto the boat. "Let's go get our kids back, guys!"

Minutes later, Red, Chuck, Bomb, and all the other birds were sailing toward Piggy Island.

As they got closer, a gray mist enveloped the boat. Through the mist the birds could see the wreckage of previous boats the pigs must have used when sailing from their island. They were all in pieces and looked like they had been abandoned for a long time. No one uttered a peep as they passed the wrecked boats.

Sometime later, the boat hit the shore of Piggy Island. Red was the first to hop off. He looked at all the nervous birds on the raft. He knew he had to take charge.

"Are you guys ready?" Red shouted. The rest of the birds roared in agreement. "Then let's go!" Red and the other Angry Birds ran up a hill that led to Pig City. When they got to the top, they could see Pig City below—and it was *enormous*! The streets were filled with houses, stores, restaurants, and food stands. The wobbly wood buildings were connected by walkways. Some structures had huge boulders on top of them, and they looked like they might collapse at any minute! Yet everything stayed upright. The birds had never seen anything like it.

Searching the city for any sign of where the eggs were being held, Red spotted a large building where there was an enormous poster of Leonard holding some of the eggs. It looked like a castle. Red realized that that must be where Leonard was, and where the eggs were being kept!

"Wow. That thing is huge," said Chuck.

Bomb nodded his agreement. "You could

fit, like, a thousand Terences in there!"

"And that's exactly where we're going," said Red.

Matilda approached the friends and looked out at Pig City.

"Do you guys remember everything you learned in my class?"

"Yup," said Red.

"Nope," said Chuck.

At the same time Bomb asked, "What class?"

Matilda shook her head. "Forget all of it for now. It's time to let loose!"

"Oh good," said Red. "Because I never learned anything anyway."

"Me neither," agreed Chuck. "I just came to socialize."

"I just came for the snacks," said Bomb.

Matilda fumed, then looked at the castle.

"How are we going to get over there?" she asked.

Red thought for a minute, then the perfect answer hit him.

"I'll tell you how. We're going to fly," he said.

Stella knew exactly what he meant. "We're going to use the slingshot!" she shouted.

Terence used all his strength to plant the slingshot in the ground while Red addressed the birds.

"Remember, the goal is to get to the castle. That's where the eggs are!" Red instructed. "Who wants to go first?"

"I do!" said Matilda. She was itching to get at the pigs for tricking her and her friends.

"Great!" said Red. "We're going to shoot you from this thing. It's going to be really fast and probably a little scary, but—"

"Shoot it!" said Matilda, interrupting Red.

Red smiled and nodded at Terence.

"Okeydoke. Fire!"

Matilda rocketed through the air and surprised everyone by releasing fireballs . . . out of her butt! She aimed directly for the pigs' houses. Soon a whole section of the city was on fire, and pigs ran in every direction.

"Take that!" she yelled. "Boom, baby, boom!"

"Wow," said Red. "I didn't know she could do that."

"Yeah, and from her butt, too," added Chuck.

Matilda landed short of the castle, so Red had another bird shot over. When that bird didn't reach the target, more birds volunteered to be slung over. None of them reached the castle. But they did their best to cause as much damage to the city as they could. The birds landed all over the city, destroying the pigs' creaky wooden structures.

Slowly the pigs noticed the Angry Birds flying toward them and crashing into their homes and stores. It finally dawned on the pigs that they were under attack! They began to panic and ran screaming from their buildings. Pigs crashed into one another on the streets. Some ran toward the castle. In just a few seconds, Pig City had erupted into utter chaos!

Back on the hill, Red was frustrated. The slingshot was not getting any of the birds close to the castle. Then Red heard a very familiar, very slimy voice, and he went from frustrated to furious.

"Citizens of Piggy Island, the birds are attacking our home!" proclaimed Leonard. His voice echoed from speakers placed throughout the city. All the pigs heard him, but so did the birds!

"Do what you must to stop them! On a separate note, I will now eat the eggs for lunch instead of dinner as originally planned!

So if you received a dinner invitation, come quickly!" he said.

Red realized that they needed an alternate plan, and fast. He spotted Terence and ran toward him.

"Terence! I've got an idea! It's risky, so I'm going to do it myself. See that giant boulder near Leonard's castle? Launch me right toward the top of that thing."

Terence grunted in agreement as Red positioned himself inside the slingshot. Red soared through the air. He curled himself into a ball, bounced off the boulder, and launched himself right at the castle! With a loud crash, Red broke through the roof. He had done it!

"I'm in!" Red shouted to Chuck and Bomb. "Send everyone else on over!"

Terence grabbed Chuck and launched him in the same direction as Red. Chuck went soaring through the air. He ramped into super-speed and hit the castle so hard he broke through the walls and some doors before landing hard next to Red.

As Chuck slowly got up, Red could see that he had a black eye, a twisted wing, and some singed feathers. Chuck shook his head and tried to clear his vision.

"Bomb is on his way," said Chuck.

Just as Chuck finished his sentence, Bomb came soaring toward them and landed with an enormous thud.

"All right," said Red. "Let's do this! Let's find those eggs!"

Leonard had had enough. How dare those birds come and take his precious eggs. They were ruining his home, too. The nerve! He had to eat the eggs before the birds could get them back—and quickly!

"Call in the Piggy Air Force," Leonard ordered. He addressed his fellow pigs through the citywide speakers. "My friends! The treacherous birds have repaid our friendship with an unprovoked act of aggression. Their attack will fail. We have TNT!"

Seconds later, a hangar door in a nearby cave opened, and several oddly shaped planes and aircraft rolled out and took to the air. Like everything the pigs made, these machines looked sloppy and barely held together. The pigs loaded the planes with TNT and tried to drop it on the birds. Mostly they missed their targets and wound up destroying their own homes and buildings! But they dropped enough TNT to make the birds retreat. The birds raced out of Pig City and scrambled back up the hill to safety.

"The birds did not figure on the courage of the pigs!" Leonard finished, then turned to Ross. "Ross!" he shouted. "Prepare the feast!"

Ross shouted instructions to the pig chef as Leonard took his seat and smiled. He sat at the head of a long banquet table with several prominent city pigs who had rushed to the castle after hearing his message. They all picked up their knives and forks and banged them on the table.

"We want eggs! We want eggs! We want eggs!" they shouted in unison.

Leonard's lips curled into an evil smile.

"Soon, my friends. Very, very soon . . ."

CHAPTER 10

Back on the hill overlooking Pig City, Terence positioned himself in front of the slingshot. He stretched the band as far as it could go, determined to give himself enough power to reach Leonard's house and help his friends. However, just as he prepared to launch himself into the air, the band snapped and the slingshot broke! Terence looked down and grunted in anger. How was he going to help his friends now?!

Meanwhile, down in Pig City, Matilda was shooting fireballs at all the pigs that she encountered. Some of the piggy guards tried to catch her. But she was too fast.

"Pop, piggies, pop!" she shouted as she went into different yoga poses and unleashed more fireballs. "Eggs-plosive!"

As the pigs scattered, Matilda beamed. Maybe it was better to be a little angry after all. She'd spent so much time squelching her angry feelings that she forgot how good it felt to let loose!

In the castle, Red, Chuck, and Bomb rounded a corner and realized they had found what they were looking for. Straight ahead was a large door with a sign on it that read NO EGGS IN HERE. There were five pigs guarding the door, too. The trio knew better by now—the pigs were not smart enough to keep the eggs truly hidden. Red quickly came up with a plan.

"Bomb, you can handle two of 'em. Chuck, I don't know if you can help. We've got to figure out a way to get into that roo—"

Before Red could finish his sentence, Chuck went into super-speed, grabbed a bucket of paint, and put it on one of the guards' heads. He took more paint and wrote I STINK! on another guard's chest, then put paint buckets on the other guards' hooves. He moved so fast that he was already back standing next to Red and Bomb as Red finished his sentence!

"—m. Does anyone have any ideas?"

At the same moment, the pig with the paint bucket on his head fell down, the one Chuck had painted on hit another pig, and the other pigs saw the paint buckets on their hooves and chased one another down the hall. The egg room was now completely unguarded!

"Wait, what the heck just happened?!" cried Red.

Chuck looked pleased with himself. "You were saying?"

The three birds ran into the room, only to see that the eggs were in a net that was being carried away on a large rope. Thinking fast, Red leaped up and grabbed onto the net as the eggs were being pulled through a large hole in the wall. Chuck and Bomb ran after him, trying to catch up as the eggs traveled through Leonard's castle.

"Hey, eggs, listen up," said Red, in an effort to reassure both himself and the eggs. "I'm here. Everything's going to be okay. We're going to get you out of here."

Before he could do anything more, Red found himself suspended above a giant caldron in Leonard's banquet hall. As he held on to the eggs for dear life, he saw Leonard and all the pigs seated at a large table below.

"What *is* this?" asked Red, confused as to what was going on.

"What is *he* doing up there?" shouted Leonard angrily.

Red realized that the pigs were going to boil the eggs and eat them, so he rushed to free them. When Leonard figured out what Red was doing, he shouted at the pig cook.

"Fine, boil *him*, too!"

Just as the eggs began to lower into the caldron full of boiling water, Red saw something large outside the window. . . .

It was Mighty Eagle!

"Hello, Red," said Mighty Eagle. "Don't worry, I got this!" With a loud cry of "MIGH-TY EA-GLE," the large bird crashed through the banquet hall windows and onto the table. But Mighty Eagle was flying too fast and kept going. He slid all the way down the table and hit his head against the caldron with a loud *BONK!* He was knocked out cold!

Red dropped onto the table next to Mighty Eagle and tried to wake him. "Mighty Eagle! Mighty Eagle, c'mon, wake up! Oof," he said, catching a whiff of Mighty Eagle's breath. "That's bad breath! Yuck!"

Leonard stomped toward the birds. He

was fed up and determined to eat the eggs without further interruption.

"Throw them *both* into the pot for seasoning!" he shouted.

Red slapped Mighty Eagle across the face a few times to get him to wake up. "C'mon, Mighty Eagle! Wake up! Wake up!"

"Don't even try," said Leonard. "You're all finished!"

"Not so fast!" shouted a voice from across the hall. It was Bomb! He and Chuck had finally caught up with Red and the eggs! At that moment, Mighty Eagle woke up, and Red knew his hero would save the day.

"Mighty Eagle! I need you to fly the eggs to safety," he pleaded.

"No worries," said Mighty Eagle. "I've got this!"

With a giant push off the table, he grabbed the net of eggs and started to make his way out of the banquet hall and into the open sky.

"My eggs!" screamed Leonard.

"Don't forget Chuck and Bomb!" shouted Red. They were waiting by the open window.

As Mighty Eagle flew past, Chuck and Bomb grabbed on to the net of eggs and were carried away. Red held on to the net as well. But Leonard pulled one of Red's legs and wouldn't let go.

"You're not going *any*where! You've ruined *everything*!" shouted Leonard.

Red was being pulled in two directions. Mighty Eagle was straining to break free and fly away with the eggs and his friends. And Leonard kept tugging at Red's leg. Then the net started to tear. A single blue egg fell down. It bounced back into the banquet hall and cracked when it hit the ground. Red knew he needed to let go in order to rescue the egg.

"Save yourselves," he told Mighty Eagle, Chuck, and Bomb. "I'm going to get that egg!"

"Red, no!" shouted Chuck, but it was too late. Red was pulled back into the banquet hall. And Mighty Eagle took off toward safety.

"Red . . . ," whispered Chuck. He started to tear up as Leonard's castle grew smaller and smaller in the distance. What was going to happen to Red, Chuck wondered. He didn't want to think about it. It hurt too much.

However, he had no time to worry, as Chuck saw the Piggy Air Force behind them. More and more planes were coming out of the hangar and down the ramp. Unless the hangar was destroyed quickly, the birds would be outnumbered and defeated.

"I've gotta blow up that ramp," said Bomb.

"No!" shouted Chuck. "It's too dangerous!"

"But I need to stop those planes!" Bomb argued, then jumped onto the nearest plane, and bounced from one to the other until he reached the ramp leading into the hangar.

"Come on, Bomb, you can do this," he said to himself. "Blow up! Blow up! Think explosive thoughts!"

As a massive piggy plane started descending the ramp right toward Bomb, the black bird realized it was now or never. He thought of surprise parties and yoga poses and, finally, of the dozens of pigs in their planes. Suddenly, a loud *BOOM* shook the hangar as Bomb exploded.

"I blew up!" Bomb shouted as he made his way back to the hill where the birds were gathered. "On purpose! Yes! I am *awesome!*"

CHAPTER 11

Back in the banquet hall, Leonard saw the cracked blue egg lying on the floor.

"Well, look at this," he said triumphantly. "I'll take that!"

"Give me that!" shouted Red as he lunged for the egg.

Both Leonard and Red missed, but Ross picked it up and prepared to toss it into the caldron.

Before Ross could throw the egg into the caldron, Red grabbed it out of Ross's hooves and held it close to him. He looked for a way to escape, then realized he was surrounded by pigs. There was no way out.

"You just don't know when to stop, do you?" asked Ross angrily. "Guards! Seize him!"

Red struggled to get away from the guards. They knocked into the caldron of boiling water, tipping it over. A tidal wave of searing hot liquid flooded the banquet hall, and the pigs scattered for cover. Red jumped up and grabbed on to the chandelier above the table. Leonard jumped up right behind him and tried to snatch the egg from Red.

"You're wrecking my castle!" yelled Leonard. "What's wrong with you?!"

"You wrecked my house!" replied Red. "Now we're even!"

Suddenly, the chandelier came loose from the ceiling and crashed to the ground, Leonard and Red falling with it. They landed far below, making a hole in the floor. Red had the wind knocked out of him, and the egg slipped from his grasp.

In another part of Pig City, Matilda and some of the other birds found themselves trapped by a giant wooden tank. It was headed straight toward them. Then the window rolled down, and Terence popped his head out. He had found a way to get to the city and save his fellow birds!

Matilda smiled and waved at Terence. "Way to go, big boy! Come on, everyone, let's go!"

Matilda and the birds climbed into the tank, and Terence steered them back toward the hill overlooking the city.

＊ ✺ ✚ ✺ ＊

"I got it," Leonard said as he snatched the egg up from the ground next to Red. "Delicious bird's egg!" He started to heat it up with a candle from the chandelier.

"You can't eat eggs!" said Red. He looked for something to use as a weapon. He saw that the room was full of TNT, and he suddenly got an idea.

"What are you going to do?" asked Leonard. "I'm a foodie!"

"Well, I guess you win," said Red.

"What?" asked Leonard.

"That was an awesome plan, to steal the eggs. We never saw it coming."

"I know!" agreed Leonard. "Who would do something like that? I mean, I would, actually!"

"True! But hey—what's that over there?"

asked Red, pointing behind Leonard.

When the pig turned to look at what Red was pointing to, Red grabbed a crate of TNT. He threw it at Leonard, who dropped the egg. Red caught it just as the crate hit the big pig. Suddenly the candle Leonard was holding ignited the dynamite inside.

"Uh-oh!" said Leonard as all around them, crates of TNT began to explode.

Back on the hillside overlooking Pig City, the birds watched and waited for signs of Red and his friends. They gasped in surprise as they saw Mighty Eagle flying toward them, the net of eggs held securely in his talons. The birds cried and cheered as Mighty Eagle landed.

Chuck, Bomb, and Terence began handing out the eggs to the birds they belonged to. Soon every set of bird parents was reunited with their eggs. All except for two birds named Olive and Greg, who were the parents of the blue egg that had been left behind—the one Red had fought so hard to save.

Before Chuck and Bomb could explain what had happened, there was a giant explosion behind them. They all turned to watch just as the castle went up in flames.

"Red!" shouted Chuck and Bomb together. They ran to the edge of the hill, desperate to see a glimpse of their friend.

"Where is he?" asked Chuck.

"C'mon, buddy, where are you?" whispered Bomb.

Even Mighty Eagle was worried that

something had happened to Red. After several very long minutes, the birds began to give up hope that their friend had made it out safely with the last egg. Bomb and Chuck would not budge from their spot. The idea that Red was gone was just too painful to bear.

All of a sudden, they spotted something moving in the castle ruins. Could it be Red? After a few seconds more, Red emerged from the rubble, the blue egg held safely in his wings. His feathers were rough and ruffled, but he was alive!

"He's alive!" shouted Chuck. "He's alive!"

The birds cheered and shouted as Red made his way up the hilltop. He gave the blue egg back to Olive and Greg, just as it cracked open to reveal three baby blue birds inside! The proud parents hugged their chicks close, and Red couldn't help but smile. He had done it. He had saved all the eggs!

Just like he'd promised.

"You made it!" shouted Chuck as he jumped up and down for joy. "Come here, pal!"

Bomb grabbed Red and pulled him into a hug. "I'm so happy to see you, buddy!"

Chuck put his wings around Red and Bomb as Red gave his friends a big squeeze.

"It's good to see you guys," said Red, and for the first time, he genuinely meant it.

Mighty Eagle approached the trio. He looked happy and relieved. "You learned your lesson well." He pulled the three birds into a big and awkward hug. "You're my prized pupils," he said proudly.

"Your prized *what*?" asked Red as Mighty Eagle released them from his grip.

"Don't you see?" Mighty Eagle said. "I had to make you lose faith in me so you could learn to have faith in yourselves!"

"That's really not how it felt," said Chuck.

"Yeah," agreed Red. "I don't think that's what happened. . . ."

"Oh look, you're blushing!" said Mighty Eagle, pointing to Red.

"I'm not blushing," said Red. "I'm just . . . red!"

In the following days, the birds rebuilt Bird Village, complete with a new and even bigger statue of Mighty Eagle in the center of the village. The statue honored Mighty Eagle's latest act of heroism, when he saved all the eggs. (Even though it was really Red who had saved the day.) After it was unveiled, Red, Chuck, and Bomb stared up at it.

"Look at that," said Chuck. "They gave Mighty Eagle all the credit. You know, back when I was angry, that would have really ticked me off."

"Ah, forget about it," said Bomb.

"You know what we should do?" asked Chuck. "Go to the beach!"

Red looked at both birds awkwardly. "Actually, I'd love to go hang out with you guys, but, you know, I've got this thing, and I have another thing after that thing, and there's all these other things as well. . . ."

Chuck and Bomb ignored Red. They started walking toward the beach. Red followed close behind. As they approached the hill overlooking the beach, Bomb stopped and smiled.

"Well, would you look at that," he said, pointing up ahead.

Red could not believe his eyes. All the birds were waiting for him on the beach, standing next to Red's hut—which had been completely rebuilt! Red was at a loss for words.

"What the . . . ?" he asked, incredulous.

Judge Peckinpah approached Red. "Mr. Red, we've rebuilt your home. We wanted to say thank you for everything you have done for us."

All the birds started cheering and applauding, and Red could not help but feel touched. Maybe being angry and alone wasn't the best way to be after all. Maybe it really was better to have friends and be a part of a community. He looked around at his friends Chuck and Bomb and realized that that was exactly what they were: his friends. And that felt pretty darn good.

Red grabbed Chuck and Bomb and gave them a big hug. As he did so, all the other birds gathered around them and clapped Red on the back.

Yeah, thought Red. *This isn't so bad after all. . . .*

EPILOGUE

"**A**nd that's how you fellas were hatched," said Red, wrapping up his story, "and how Bird Island survived the pigs' attack." He looked over at the three blue birds, who were getting drowsy.

"We're so happy you saved all of us," said Jake as he yawned and turned over in the nest.

"Yeah," agreed Jay. "We think you're awesome, Uncle Red."

"We love you, Uncle Red," said Jim. His eyes closed, and soon he was fast asleep.

"I love you, too, guys," whispered Red as he tiptoed out of the room and let the blue birds drift off to sleep.

As he made his way back to his hut, Red couldn't get over how much his life had changed in such a short amount of time. Once he felt alone and angry, and now he felt like he was a part of life on Bird Island. He had friends, he had a purpose, and he had a beautiful new home. He was even a little happy every now and then.

Red stopped to watch the last bit of sun set over the ocean. Just then a fly buzzed by. It went round and round his head. Red swatted it away and ended up smacking himself in the beak!

Red kicked the sand and felt a little better. Underneath it all, he would always be an Angry Bird. It was just his nature. And truth be told, Red was okay with that. It was kind of his thing.